Philipp Winterberg   Nadja Wichmann

Ako ba ay maliit?
Am I small?

AVAILABLE FOR EVERY COUNTRY ON EARTH
IN AT LEAST ONE OFFICIAL LANGUAGE

Filipino/Tagalog (Wikang Filipino/Tagalog)
English (English)

Translation (Filipino/Tagalog): Kristel Aquino-Estanislao
Translation (English): Philipp Winterberg, Sandra Hamer and David Hamer

Text/Publisher: Philipp Winterberg, Münster, www.philippwinterberg.com · Illustrations: Nadja Wichmann · Fonts: Patua One, Noto Sans etc. · Photos: Philipp Winterberg, Lena Hesse etc. · Translation: Heidi Alatalo, Mica Allalouf, Kristel Aquino-Estanislao, Manuel Bernal Márquez, Sanja Bulatović, Jingyi Chen, Aminath Mohamed Didi, Rudolf-Josef Fischer, Renate Glas, Elspeth Grace Hall, Sandra Hamer, Shahzaman Haque, Tania Hoffmann-Fettes, Sabina Hona, Joo Yeon Kang, Şebnem Karakaş, Galina Konstantinovna Zakharova, Chi Le, Kristina Mørch Hendriksen, Alina Omhandoro, Marisa Pereira Paço Pragier, Myat Pyi Phyo, Voara Ralaiarijaona, Mialy Razanajatovo, Juga Réka, Saeid Samar, Fiona Sindhikara, Katarina Stock, Iliriana Bisha Tagani, Tshering Tashi, Andreanna Tatsi, Daryna Temerbek, Lobsang Tsering, Laurence Wuillemin etc.

Ito si Tamia.

This is Tamia.

**Tama!
Eksakto!**

Right!
Exactly!

Si Tamia ay maliit na maliit pa.

Tamia is still very small.

Ako?
Maliit?

Me?
Small?

Ako ba ay maliit?
Am I small?

Maliit? Ikaw? Ikaw ay mas maliit pa sa maliit! Ikaw ay napakaliit!

Small? You? You are smaller than small! You are teeny-weeny!

**Mumunti? Ikaw?
Ikaw ay napakamunti!**

Mini? You?
You are tiny!

Ako ba ay mumunti?
Am I mini?

Ako ba ay napakamunti?

Am I tiny?

Napakamunti? Ikaw?
Ikaw ay katiting!

Tiny? You?
You are microscopic!

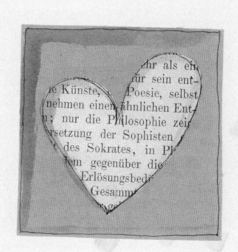

Ako ba ay katiting?

Am I microscopic?

**Katiting? Ikaw?
Ikaw ay malaki!**

Microscopic? You?
You are big!

Ako ba ay malaki?

Am I big?

Malaki? Ikaw?
Ikaw ay malaking-malaki!

Big? You?
You are large!

Ako ba ay malaking-malaki?

Am I large?

**Malaking-malaki? Ikaw?
Ikaw ay napakalaki!**

Large? You?
You are huge!

Ako ba ay napakalaki?

Am I huge?

**Napakalaki? Ikaw?
Ikaw ay higante!**

Huge? You?
You are gigantic!

...at kung ako ay lahat,
ako rin ay: sakto lang!

...and if I'm everything,
I'm also: just right!

Many thanks to all translators!

Mastewal Abera, Tirea Aean, Heidi Alatalo, Mica Allalouf, Rizky Ranny Andayani, Kristel Aquino-Estanislao, Amila Lakshitha Ariyarathna, Senggé Aslan, Andy Ayres, Hroviland Bairhteins, Rajneesh Bhardwaj, Christa Blattmann, Manuel Bernal Márquez, Arrah Brown, Sanja Bulatović, Jingyi Chen, Aminath Mohamed Didi, Tanja Dolinšek, Sumiyabaatar Enkhbaatar, Alejandro Escobedo, Edmund Fairfax, Meliha Fazlic, Rudolf-Josef Fischer, Stephen Gadd, Merrymel George, Renate Glas, Anta Gramm, Sallehuddin Hadi, Tony Hak, Elspeth Grace Hall, David Hamer, Sandra Hamer, Shahzaman Haque, Wiremu Henley, Tania Hoffmann-Fettes, Maryam Holton, Sabina Hona, Petr Hrabe, Tamara Hveisel Hansen, Laura Iglesias Padrón, Liliana Ioan, Akira Ikegami, Farkhod Isaev, Firuz Jumaev, Joo Yeon Kang, Şebnem Karakaş, Galina Konstantinovna Zakharova, Jahan Kos, Anjali Kshirsagar, Irina Kuhtarskih, Dhiraj Kumar, Chi Le, Roy Lin, Niru Liyanaarachchi, Steaphan MacRisnidh, Ruhana Mammadova, Arwa Marwan-Bakr, Mustafa Masoomi, Cheikh M. Mbengue, Majda Mchiche, Kristina Mørch Hendriksen, Ľudmila Košková Nesbit, Henry Kow Nyadiah, Darán Ó Dochartaigh, Fred Mokaya Omangi, Alina Omhandoro, Goran Pavlicevic, Marisa Pereira Paço Pragier, Kheng Piseth, Lusine Poghosyan, Shankar Prasad, Myat Pyi Phyo, H. K. Raghavendra, R. Rajamanickam, Voara Ralaiarijaona, Subramanian Ramaswamy, Mialy Razanajatovo, Juga Réka, María Remírez Balloqui, Dmitriy Rokhlin, Antonella Rosini, Zarina Sadyrbek, Frank Sam, Saeid Samar, Bongiwe Segasa, Aarav Shah, Aaron Crow Simon, Fiona Sindhikara, Bouakeo Sivilay, Katarina Stock, Inara Tabir, Iliriana Bisha Tagani, Pola Taisali, Tshering Tashi, Andreanna Tatsi, Gary Taylor-Raebel, Daryna Temerbek, Lyubomir Tomov, Lobsang Tsering, Mai-Le Timonen Wahlström, Varuwa Vandi, Milica Vranjanac, An Wielockx, Gifty Claresa Wiafe, Isaac Wekesa Wangila, Chor-Tung Wong, Laurence Wuillemin, Yolanda Wu etc.

A World Children's Book for Every Country on the Planet

From Afar to Zulu: The picture book *Am I small?* has been translated into over 100 languages since its publication.

The story by author Philipp Winterberg is available for every country in the world in at least one national language. It is the world's first children's book covering the entire globe.

In *Am I small?* young and old readers alike accompany the girl Tamia on a journey full of wonders. Together they discover that size is relative and that Tamia is just right the way she is. "Enchanting" judges the trade journal *Eselsohr*; "wonderful for bilingual families, and kindergartens," says the *Börsenblatt* and the book review magazine *Kirkus Reviews* kindly compliments "for children who enjoy lingering over pages full of magical creatures and whimsical details [...] told in simple and engaging words and imaginative pictures."

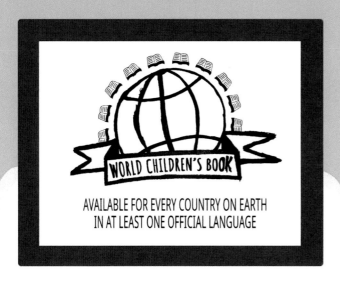

AVAILABLE FOR EVERY COUNTRY ON EARTH
IN AT LEAST ONE OFFICIAL LANGUAGE

More than 200 translators have already participated in the World Children's Book. Sometimes the research took months, "I had to look for a Tibetan translator for almost a year," says Winterberg. The book is now also available in thousands of language combinations, such as Arabic-Tagalog or Portuguese-Tigrinya — a language spoken in Ethiopia and Eritrea, whose script is reminiscent of children's drawings.

In the years and decades to come the World Children's Book project will continue to grow. The aim is to gradually translate *Am I small?* into over 500 languages.

Many thanks to all readers!

About the Author...

Philipp B. Winterberg M.A. studied Communication Science, Psychology and Law. He lives in Berlin and loves being multifaceted: He went parachuting in Namibia, meditated in Thailand, and swam with sharks and stingrays in Fiji and Polynesia.

Philipp Winterberg's books introduce new perspectives on essential themes like friendship, mindfulness and happiness. They are read in languages and countries all over the globe.

■ MORE ■ MÁS ■ DI PIÙ ■ PLUS ■ MEHR ■
WWW.PHILIPPWINTERBERG.COM